Not Now,

by Jennifer Schieber and Cynthia Swain • illustrated by John Speirs

"Rosa, here is your
new baby brother," said Mom.
"His name is Carlos. Come and
see him." Rosa was excited to see
her new baby brother.

Mom asked Rosa if she would like to hold the baby. Rosa was very excited. She had never held a baby before.

Rosa's dog, Sam, started barking. He wanted Rosa to hold him, too. "No, Sam," said Rosa. "Not now."

Mom asked Rosa if she would like to feed the baby. Rosa was excited. She had never fed a baby before.

Sam came over with his dish.
He wanted Rosa to feed him, too.
"No, Sam," said Rosa. "Not now."

Mom wanted to take the baby for a walk. She asked Rosa if she would like to push the stroller. Rosa was excited!

Sam came over with his leash.
He wanted to go for a walk, too.
Rosa almost said, "No, Sam.
Not now." But she didn't.

They all went for a walk.